On Market Street

On Market Street

Pictures by
Anita Lobel
Words by Arnold Lobel

Scholastic Inc.
New York Toronto London Auckland Sydney Tokyo

ISBN 0-590-40299-4

Text copyright © 1981 by Arnold Lobel.
Illustrations copyright © 1981 by Anita Lobel.
All rights reserved. This edition published by
Scholastic Inc., 730 Broadway, New York, NY 10003,
by arrangement with Greenwillow Books.

12 11 10 9 8 7 6 5 4 3 2 1   5 6 7 8 9 9/8 0/9

Printed in the U.S.A.   09

To Timothy and Susan Benn

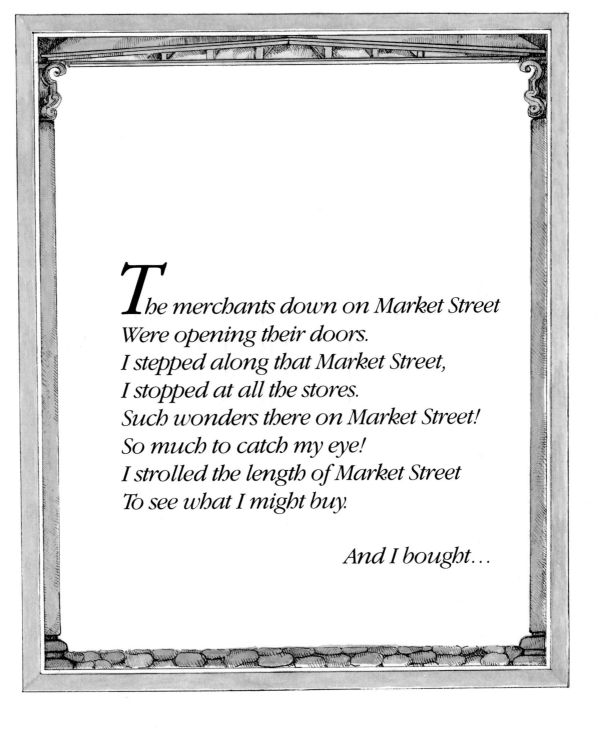

The merchants down on Market Street
Were opening their doors.
I stepped along that Market Street,
I stopped at all the stores.
Such wonders there on Market Street!
So much to catch my eye!
I strolled the length of Market Street
To see what I might buy.

And I bought…

A

apples,

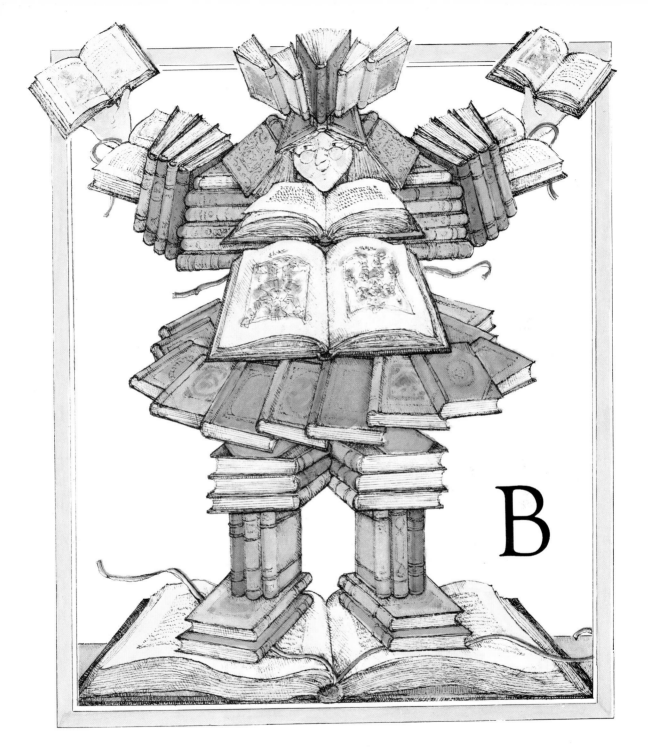

books,

clocks,

doughnuts,

eggs,

flowers,

gloves,

H

hats,

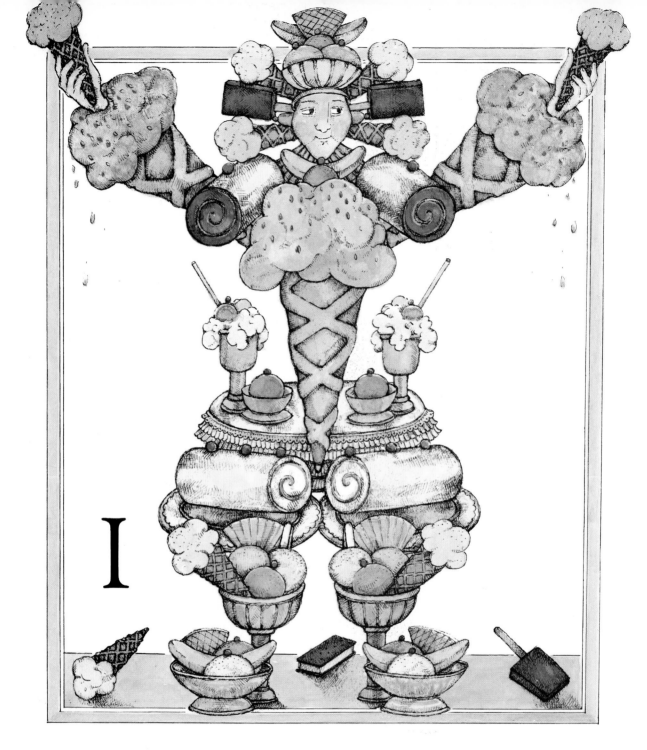

I

ice cream,

jewels,

K

kites,

lollipops,

M

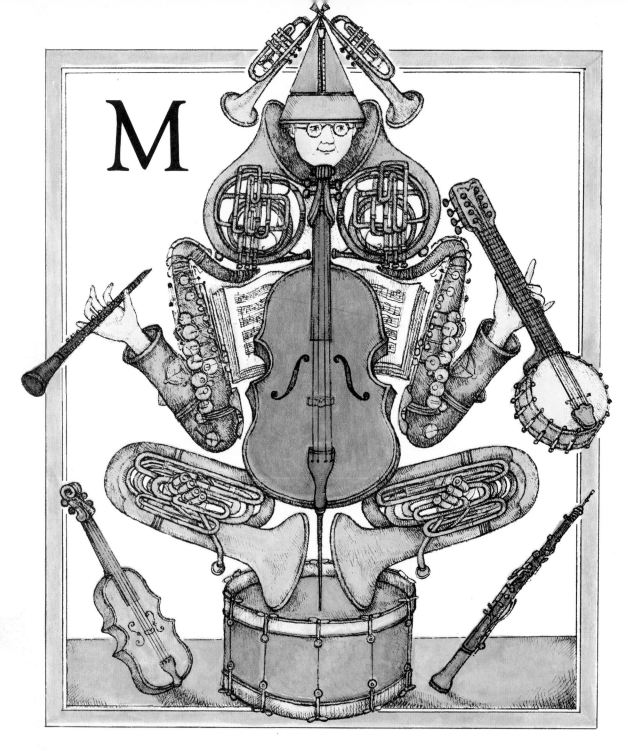

musical instruments,

noodles,

oranges,

P

playing cards,

quilts,

ribbons,

shoes,

toys,

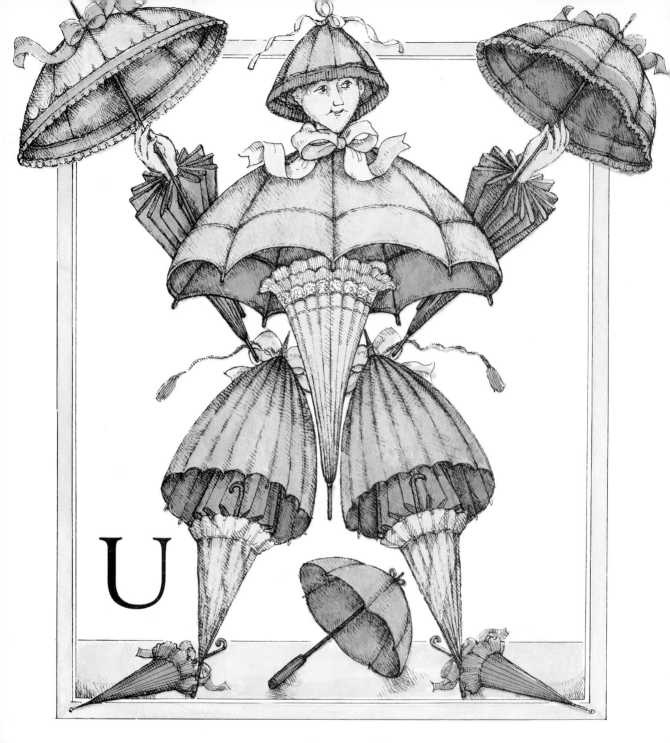

U

umbrellas,

vegetables,

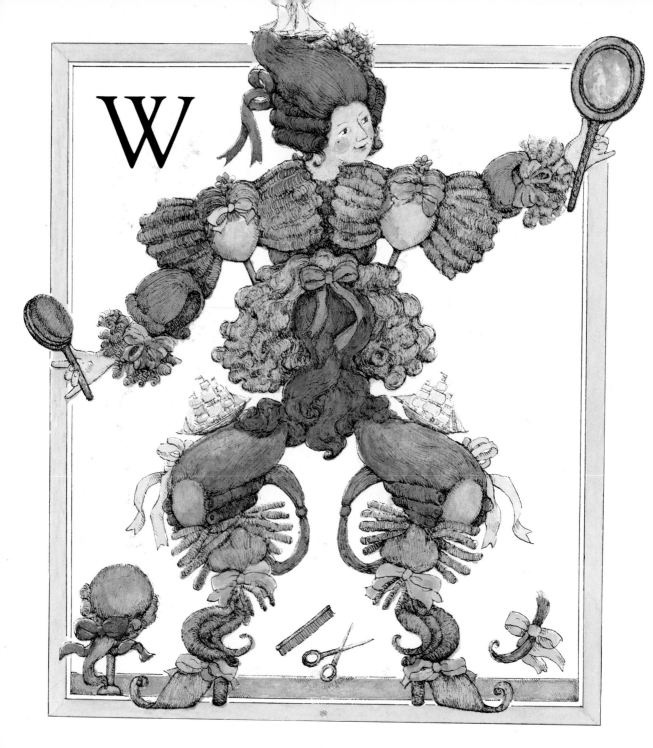

wigs,

Xmas trees,

yarns,

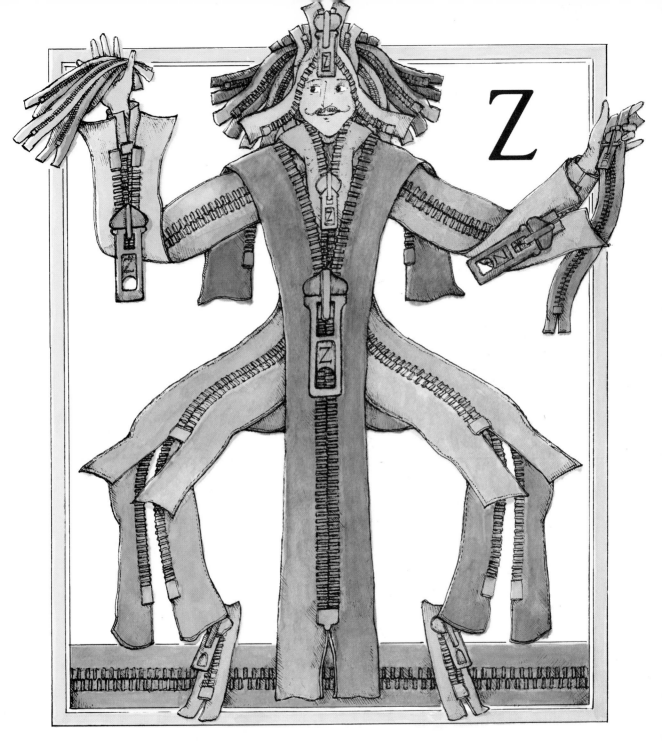

zippers.

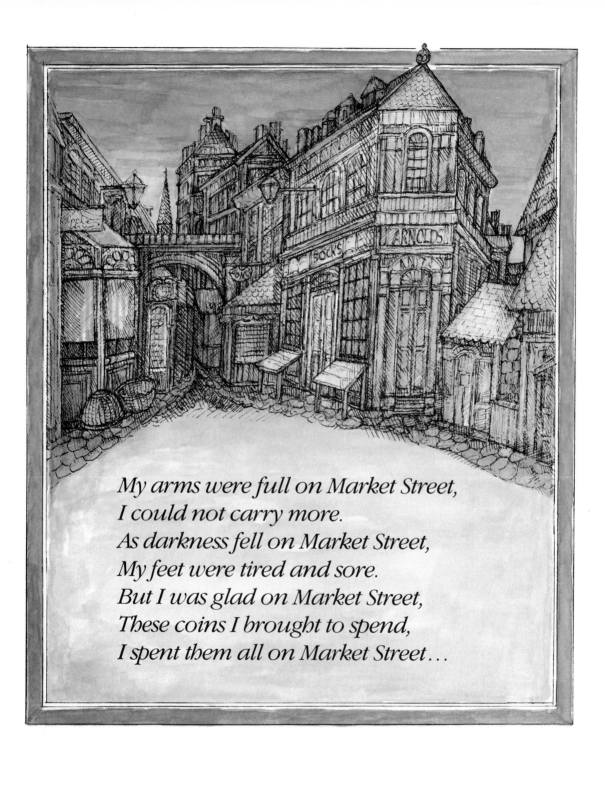

My arms were full on Market Street,
I could not carry more.
As darkness fell on Market Street,
My feet were tired and sore.
But I was glad on Market Street,
These coins I brought to spend,
I spent them all on Market Street…

...on presents for a friend.